Linoleum Blownapart

Puns, Riddles, Shaggy Dog Tales, And Mercifully Few Dad Jokes

Jan Kowski

ISBN: 9798591994747

TABLE OF CONTENTS

INTRODUCTION

In the early days of the Internet and email, friends with lots of time on their hands would regularly send emails with jokes, puns, and funny stories. Being the memory-challenged person that I am, I saved them so that I could enjoy them later. And one of the benefits of being memory-challenged, after a few months, I could go back to read them again and enjoy them all over again as if it were the first time.

I saved the best, and over the years, this became quite a collection, and that has become the core of this book.   I hope you get the laughs I did out of these, and if you have a memory like mine, you can get those laughs over and over again.

CHAPTER 1

THE GREAT QUESTIONS OF LIFE

Some things in life just don't make sense. And some things we just take for granted and we never think twice about them. Here are some of great questions in life to make you wonder and ponder. That's only if you have a really lot of time on your hands.

***

Just wondering . . . Could a lot of gunfights in the Wild West have been avoided if cowboy architects just made the towns big enough for everyone?

***

If someone accuses you of being argumentative, how do you defend yourself without proving them right?

***

Where do forest rangers go when they want to get away from it all?

***

Have you ever thought about that the Secretary of the Interior is in charge of the outdoors?

***

Do regular dogs see police dogs and think: "Oh no, it's a cop!"

***

I wonder if the guy that came up with the phrase "One Hit Wonder" ever had any other popular thoughts.

***

If all is not lost, then where the heck is it?

***

Wouldn't it be ironic if Popeye's Chicken was fried in olive oil?

***

Do twins ever realize that one of them is unplanned?

***

Is there ever a day that mattresses are not on sale?

***

Are rhinos just unicorns who have let themselves go?

***

If I take care of chickens, am I a chicken tender?

***

Why is 'abbreviated' such a long word?

***

Why do meteors always land in craters?

***

If a parsley farmer is sued, will they garnish his wages?

***

If a priest makes a mistake, is that a clerical error?

***

Have you ever thought it odd that only one company makes the game "Monopoly?"

***

If you don't pay an exorcist, do you get repossessed?

***

If your dentist fills the wrong tooth, is it acci-dental?

***

So, what is wrong with clouds one through eight?

***

Why are they called apartments when they are all stuck together?

***

Here is a thought for the day: Why don't you ever see the headline 'Psychic Wins Lottery'?

***

Why is it that banks keep their vault doors open, but chain pens to the counter?

***

If one fowl is a goose, but two are called geese, shouldn't the plural of moose be meese?

***

Why do we have noses that run and feet that smell?

***

How many Lowe's could Rob Lowe rob if Rob Lowe could rob Lowe's?

***

**Do chiropractors get back pay?

***

What if there were no hypothetical questions?

***

If a man had a secret life as a priest, would that be his altar eg0

***

We have fingertips, but not toe tips. So why do we tiptoe, but not tipfinger?

***

Cough, Rough, Though, Through. Why in the world don't these words rhyme? But for some reason pony and bologna do.

***

If man evolved from monkeys and apes, why do we still have monkeys and apes?

***

CHAPTER 2

THE WORLD WOULD BE A BUTTER PLACE

Word Play . . . being clever with the twists and turns and nuances of the English language. Word play sounds like an intellectual exercise for smart people, doesn't it? But it's really just a sneaky way of saying that this is a collection of really, really clever puns.

I have been diagnosed with sausagephobia. I always fear the wurst.

***

What do a dog and a cell phone have in common? Both have Collar ID.

***

My friend failed the exam to become a magician. Too many trick questions.

***

This morning I could hear music coming from my printer. I went to investigate, and found that it was the paper jamming.

***

If only we could get rid of margarine . . . the world would be a butter place.

My cousin is a social vegan. He avoids meet

***

It was really crowded at Legoland last weekend. People were lined up for blocks.

***

I have a friend who is so lazy he puts popcorn in his pancakes so they will turn over by themselves.

***

A dermatologist friend plans to open his own practice. He's starting from scratch. I told him that was a rash decision.

***

I had a bunch of puns about milk, but my wife doesn't like them. I guess she's laughtose intolerant.

***

Went to the zoo yesterday. Saw a baguette in a cage. Must have been bread in captivity.

***

A new study reports that a dog can retrieve a stick from over a half-mile away. That seems a bit far-fetched to me.

***

I tried to catch some fog. I mist.

***

There's a report that vandals have attacked the origami museum in Tokyo. We'll keep you updated as the story unfolds.

***

No matter how much music changes through the years, AC/DC will always be current.

***

Rejection comes from those who no you.

***

Someone's dog pooped on the sidewalk, and they didn't clean it up. I call that a dereliction of doodie.

***

I should have been sad when my flashlight batteries died. But I was delighted.

***

   A rabbit was at the dentist for a tooth extraction. When the dentist told the rabbit he would be using

***

Novocain as an anesthetic, the rabbit jumped up and said: "You can't do that! I'm the ether bunny!"

***

My wife is doubting my ability to repair household electrical appliances. Well, she's in for a shock.

***

The former child actor Buckwheat has converted to Islam. He has changed his name . . . to Kareem of Wheat.

***

My favorite folk song from the sixties is "Blowing in the wind" by Peter Pollen Mary.

***

I have a friend who was always complaining about the repairs to his little Swedish car. It was one Saab story after another.

***

I dreamed I was eating Altoids that tasted like Fig Newtons. I guess it was just a fig mint of my imagination.

***

The only thing flat-earthers have to fear . . . is sphere itself.

***

Bread is a lot like the sun. It rises in the yeast, and sets in the waist.

***

Trying to enroll in harp school, but it's tough. I'll have to pull a few strings to get in. (Like my friend who enrolled in marionette school.)

***

Great Britain doesn't have a kidney bank . . . but they do have a Liverpool.

***

I love bad jokes about eyes. The cornea, the better.

***

Her: Are you aware of the fact that Thailand used to have a different name?
Me: Yes, Siam.

***

Chromosome report:
XX = Male;
XY = Female;
YYY = Delilah

***

A slice of apple pie is $2.00 in Jamaica. It is $2.50 in the Bahamas. These are the pie rates of the Caribbean.

***

Today's definition - Bigamist: Italian fog.

***

I really admire my pharmacist. He's a piller of the community.

***

I was wrong when I thought my chiropractor was untalented. I stand corrected.

***

Yesterday, I slipped on the library floor. I guess I was in the non-friction section.

***

It only costs pirates two dollars to get their ears pierced. Buccaneer.

***

I'm going to study lock-picking for a new career. I think it will open a lot of doors for me.

***

3 AM in an electrician's home:
Wife: "Wire you insulate?"
Electrician: "Watt's it to you? I'm ohm, aren't I?"

***

Found a snake in the back yard last night. Measured it. It was 3.14159265 feet long. Must have been a pi-thon.

***

A friend of mine told me he did not understand what cloning was. I told him: "That makes two of us."

***

A scientist is packaging a set of tools and instructions for cloning deer. Calling it a Doe It Yourself Kit.

***

Never buy flowers from a monk. Only YOU can prevent florist friars.

***

My friend who has quadruplets is surprised they're always wandering off. I told her it was a four gone conclusion.

***

I am really grateful that my friend explained the word "plethora." It means a lot.

***

My friend asked me what I thought about his invention of a glass coffin. My response: "Remains to be seen."

***

Breaking news: Hundreds of hares have escaped from the zoo. Reports are that police are combing the area.

***

It's easy to convince ladies not to eat Tide pods, but it's harder to deter gents.

***

I saw a concert of killer whales.
It was well orca-strated

***

A herd of cattle got into a marijuana field in Colorado. After being removed, they again broke through the fence and returned to the field.
I guess it was a case of the pot calling the cattle back.

***

Officers were called to investigate a herd of sheep that had fallen down a hill. They reported it as a lambslide.

***

Police arrested a man on suspicion of killing a bunch of crows. There was little evidence, but probable caws.

***

There is news that police have arrested a gang of mimes. They report that they did unspeakable crimes.

***

The term for making mistakes when texting in the cold: typothermia.

***

I started a business in my home building yachts. Sails are going through the roof. But my wife says it's a hull of a way to make a living.

***

I watched a documentary on how ships are put together. It was riveting.

***

It's easy to convince ladies not to eat Tide pods, but it's harder to deter gents.

***

I'd like to give some sage advice. It goes well with parsley, rosemary and thyme.

***

Stock market report: Helium was up, feathers were down and paper was stationary.

***

News Update: A shepherd was driving his flock of sheep through town, but got a traffic ticket for making a ewe turn.

***

My not-so-bright friend read something about tectonic plates and asked me if they were dishwasher safe.
I replied: "only if you served Continental breakfast on them." I know, I know. That's faulty humor.

***

A pun has not completely matured until it is full groan.

***

Yesterday, I found a small stone that was in the shape of a guitar pick. I guess it was for rock music.

***

I'm going to write a song about tortillas. It'll be wrap music.

***

My friend went bald years ago, but still carries around an old comb with him. He just can't part with it.

***

There's a new restaurant that specializes in exotic game like baked cheetah and fried gazelle. I don't plan to eat there, though, because I'm giving up fast food.

***

I spent $300 to rent a limousine, then found that does not include a driver. I can't believe we spent that much money, and have nothing to chauffeur it.

***

No one knows how the fire started in the Notre Dame cathedral, but there's a man named Quasimodo who has a hunch.

***

My Russian friend thinks he should be an Uber driver because of his name: Pickup Andropov.

***

I know the meaning of "Adios" and "Au Revoir." I guess that makes me Bye-Lingual.

***

I tried to take some high-resolution photos of wheat fields but they all turned out grainy.

***

Some of my old coin collector friends are having a reunion. We're getting together for old dimes' sake.

***

Technology is advancing everywhere. Sheep herders are no longer using branding to identify their sheep. They have a new system of black and white vertical lines. They're calling them baaa codes.

***

A photon walked into a hotel with no luggage and went to check in. The bellhop asked if he has any bags. The photon replied, "no sir; I'm traveling light."

***

When you clean out a vacuum cleaner. . . that makes you a vacuum cleaner.

***

Here's a pun for all you mind readers . . .

***

Orthopedic surgeons get all the breaks.

***

I'm reading a romance novel in Braille. It's a touching story.

***

Narcissists are known for their wonderful I sight.

***

Scientists have discovered how trees communicate. They bark.

***

Don't run with bagpipes. You could put an aye out. Or worse yet, you could get kilt.

***

I hear that a wizard just got a job as a chef because he was good at saucery.

***

There's a new association for the ambidextrous. People are joining left and right.

***

I hear that they need help at the T-Rex Cafe. It seems that they are short-handed.

***

There was a huge fight at a seafood restaurant. Battered fish everywhere.

***

Two priests got into a fight at church. Witnesses say it was quite an altar-cation.

***

I am slowly but surely assembling a polka band. It's all going accordion to plan.

***

My friend says all four of his sons have told him they want to be valets when they grow up. He says it's the worst case of parking sons disease he has ever seen.

***

An inscription found beneath ancient Rome: Make Rome grape again. (They came, they saw, they Concord.)

***

I went shopping for cherries and a microphone stand the other day. Bought a bing, bought a boom.

***

Today I saw an ad on Craigslist that said "Radio for sale, $5, volume stuck on full." I thought to myself: "I can't turn that down."

***

A man recently rushed into a busy doctor's office and shouted, "Doctor! You have to see me now! I think I'm shrinking!"
The doctor calmly responded, "Now, settle down. You'll just have to be a little patient."

***

Do frogs wear open toad shoes?

***

People are usually shocked when they find out I am not a very good electrician.

***

People who can't distinguish between etymology and entomology bug me in ways I can't put into words.

***

There's a report that scientists have successfully grown human vocal chords in a petri dish. The results speak for themselves.

***

Schick has finally brought out a razor for dyslexics. It's the best thing since sliced beard.

***

An indecisive surgeon just won't cut it.

***

If you aren't up to the job of being a strength trainer, do you give a too weak notice?

***

I've always felt at home in water . . . ever since I was a little buoy.

***

Notice on a shoe repair shop: "I'll heel you, I'll save your sole, I'll even gladly dye for you."

***

They're planning on building a restaurant on Mars. They say the food will be great, but they're worried about a lack of atmosphere.

***

I can handle algebra, trigonometry, and calculus...but geometry is where I draw the line.

***

Whiteboards are remarkable.

***

Did you hear about the lady who backed into the power saw? Disaster.

***

People keep telling me to stop impersonating a flamingo. I guess I'll have to put my foot down.

***

I went to a terrible classical music concert. The musicians made so many mistakes I can't even begin to Liszt them. It was too much for me to Handel so I left and demanded all my money Bach the next day.

***

I'm working on a Local Area Network in Australia. I call it the LAN down under.

***

I've been trying to come up with carpentry puns that woodwork.
You know the drill.
I didn't want to screw it up.
I came up with one and thought I had nailed it.
But no one saw it.

***

A grenade thrown into a kitchen in France would result in Linoleum Blownapart.

***

Couldn't help but ask when I saw a guy with a toothbrush in his lapel. It was his class pin. He went to Colgate.

***

There are a lot of jokes about toilet paper going around.
I don't find them very Charmin.
It's Scott to stop.
This is Northern to laugh about!
I think this is some sort of vast 2-ply conspiracy.
It's very hard to absorb it all.
Thinking about it just wipes me out.
I guess I'll just have to roll along with everyone else.
I have to go now. I am getting so angry I am feeling flush.

***

Last night I dreamed I was a muffler. This morning I woke up exhausted.

***

To the person who took my ladder, return it immediately, or further steps will be taken.

***

Yesterday, at a restaurant, my friend got ketchup splashed in his eyes. He says he couldn't see a thing in front of him, but had good Heinz-sight.

***

My friend fell into a vat of curdled milk. He was in whey over his head.

***

I went to the bakery and asked for shortbread. They said they didn't make it any longer.

***

I lost my job as a stage designer. I wasn't happy about it, but I left without making a scene.

***

I saw a group of 10 ants running around frantically in my kitchen. I felt compassion for them, so I made

them a home out of a small cardboard box. I guess
that makes me their landlord, and that makes them
my . . . . tenants.

***

There are reports today of an explosion at a cheese
factory in France. Da Brie is everywhere.

***

Not all math puns are funny. Just sum.

***

Went to a Halloween party dressed as a harp.
Friend: "Your harp costume is too small"
Me: "Are you calling me a lyre?"

***

I visited a cornfield this weekend . . .
My wife was with me. She was wearing a crop-top.
It was an a-maize-ing experience
It was earie.
We thought we were being stalked.
Aw shucks.
It was just a Husky.
This is one of my best stories - cream of the crop.

Has some pop to it.
But don't believe any of it. Not a kernel of truth in it.

***

What is Dracula's favorite holiday after Halloween?
Fangs-giving.

***

My friend swallowed an alarm clock. He's experiencing some alarming side effects.

***

If you can't tie a knot then you cannot. If you can then you can knot.

***

I was going down the road hopelessly, without skill or purpose, and sure enough, I got pulled over and ticketed.
"What's the charge?", I asked.
"Feckless driving.", said the officer.

***

My wife wasn't happy when she found out I replaced our bed with a trampoline. She hit the roof.

***

A friend tells me: It's a 5-minute walk from my house to the pub. It's a 35-minute walk from the pub to my house. The difference is staggering.

***

I tried to sue the airline for misplacing my luggage. I lost my case.

***

Evidence has been found that William Tell and his family were avid bowlers. Unfortunately, all the Swiss league records were destroyed in a fire, ... and so we'll never know for whom the Tells bowled.

***

I've been diagnosed with a chronic fear of giants. It's a classic case of Fee-fi-phobia

***

The other day, I yelled into a colander. I strained my voice.

***

Whoever coined the term "emotional baggage" missed an opportunity. It should have been "griefcase."

***

I went to the pet shop and asked for twelve bees. The shopkeeper counted out thirteen and gave them to me. I pointed out that he gave me too many, and he replied: "That one is a freebee."

***

A pony was giving a speech in a lecture hall. A man in the back told him to speak up because he couldn't hear. The pony replied: "You'll have to excuse me, I'm a little horse".

***

Childhood injuries: falling off the bike, falling out of a tree.
Adult injuries: sleeping wrong; sitting too long; sneezing

***

A prison inmate had his prosthetic leg confiscated after he used it in a brawl with another prisoner. When the inmate found out the authorities were taking away his leg, he was reported to be hopping mad.

***

A friend of mine accidentally ran through a screen door . . . He strained himself.

***

Cat puns freak meowt.

***

My friend lost his job in an orange juice factory.
Got canned.
Couldn't concentrate.

***

What's in a honeymoon salad: Lettuce alone.

***

Another friend got fired from a calendar factory. All he did was take a day off.

***

I read that more people are choosing cremation over traditional burial. I guess it shows that they are thinking out of the box.

***

I like European food so I thought I would Russia over there because I was Hungary. After Czech'ing the menu, I ordered Turkey. When I was Finnished, I told the waiter, 'Spain good but there is Norway I could eat another bite.

***

Every morning I think about having pancakes, but I keep waffling.

***

Archaeologist: a person whose career lies in ruins.

***

A chicken crossing the road is poultry in motion.

***

I went to a seafood gym last week . . . And pulled a mussel.

***

I finally figured out why Waldo always wears stripes. He doesn't want to be spotted.

***

In ancient Rome, deli workers were told that they could eat anything they wanted during the lunch hour. Anything, that is except the smoked salmon. Thus were created the world's first anti-lox breaks.

***

I have a friend who thinks he's an abacus. I know he's a little weird, but I can count on him.

***

There's music coming out of my printer. I think the paper's jamming again.

***

My gnu years resolution is to tell you a gazelleon times how much I caribou you! Sorry for the bad animal puns. Alpaca bag and leave.

***

I should have been sad when my flashlight batteries died, but I was delighted.

***

I used to be addicted to the hokey-pokey, but I turned myself around.

***

A New Year's resolution is something that goes in one year and out the other.

***

My not-so-bright friend tried to cross breed a dog with a chicken. He wanted to get pooched eggs?

***

A friend of mine said he walked into a bar and asked for a pitcher full of beer, and a smart-alec bartender pointed him to a drunken baseball player.

***

This post is unrelated to elephants. I guess you could say it is irrelephant.

***

I am applying for a job at the Bicycle Wheel Manufacturers Association. They need a new spokesperson.

***

More additions to my reading library . . .
'Antibiotics' by Penny Sillin
'Art and Culture' by Phyllis Stein
'Back Problems' by Eileen Bent
'American Breakfast' by Chris P. Bacon and
'Pancakes' by Mabel Sirrup
'American Independence' by Bertha Venation
'Amphibians' by Newt and Sally Mander

***

I hear that James Bond once slept right through an earthquake. I guess you could say he was shaken, not stirred.

***

I've been thinking of learning origami. I hear that the benefits are many fold.

***

I just got off the scale. Very disappointed. Apparently, fasting has nothing to do with the speed that you eat.

***

I've ripped my feather quilt and now I'm feeling down.

***

I just tripped over a very small encyclopedia, proving that a little knowledge can be a dangerous thing.

***

I've ordered some German food over the internet; the sauerkraut has arrived but the wurst is yet to come.

***

There's a new bakery with a sense of humor. They only bake wry bread.

***

There's a report that a hardware store was burglarized and the only thing stolen was a ladder. When asked about the investigation, the owner responded: "No further steps will be taken."

***

My family told me to stop telling Thanksgiving jokes, but I told them I couldn't quit cold turkey.

***

When old carpenters retire, they just lumber around.

***

Heard in a pet store . . .
Customer: "I want to get a dog."
Pet store owner: "Sure, we have several. What kind of demeanor?"
Customer: "I want a guard dog. Da meaner, da better."

***

New historical artifacts have been discovered in rural England that show that King Arthur's round table was built by Sir Cumference.

It was first used as a dessert table. And they served . . . you guessed it . . . pi.

***

I used to be addicted to soap, but I'm clean now.

***

My friend wants to buy a motorcycle that he can ride around laughing on. I told him to buy a Yamahaha.

***

My friend is studying the history of snakes. I guess you could call him a hisssssstorian.

***

When musical notes get in treble, bass-ically they get put behind bars. The alto-nate punishment is to push them off a clef and hope they land flat on sharp objects.

***

A friend of mine is thinking about going to a Halloween party as Medusa. She thinks everyone will be petrified.

***

Warning. Don't look at the eclipse through a colander. It will strain your eyes.

***

The invisible man got a job offer. He turned it down . . . . Couldn't see himself doing it.

***

Boy: Daddy, can you tell me what an eclipse is?
Father: No sun.

***

I saw a sign at an Optometrist's Office that read: "If you don't see what you're looking for, you've come to the right place."

***

Last week, it rained cats and dogs. I stepped in a poodle.

***

My friend had a bad case of kleptomania. So, he took something for it.

***

I'm writing a novel about 2,000 mockingbirds. I think I'll call it: "Two kilomockingbirds."

***

I'm designing a t-shirt with rows of corn printed on it. I think I'll call it a crop-top.

***

An egotist is someone who is usually me-deep in conversation.

***

The power company would be delighted if you send in your payment. However, if you don't, you will be.

***

A famous Viking explorer returned home from a voyage and found his name missing from the town register.

His wife insisted on complaining to the local civic official who apologized profusely saying, "I must have taken Leif off my census."

***

My room mates are concerned that I'm using their kitchen utensils, but that's a whisk I'm willing to take.

***

I've been trying to make a pun about quicksand but I'm stuck.

***

I invented a new device to assist farmers in keeping track of the size of their herds.
I think I'll call it . . . a cow-culator.

***

A criminal's best asset is his lie-ability

***

I had to check my pet duck into rehab. He's a quack addict.

***

My friend makes end of the world jokes like there's no tomorrow.

***

If a judge loves the sound of his own voice, expect a long sentence.

***

In my opinion, 6:30 is the best time on a clock, hands down.

Linoleum Blownapart

CHAPTER 3

MORE OF LIFE'S GREAT QUESTIONS, WITH
ANSWERS THIS TIME

Okay, okay. They're not life's greatest questions. They're really just a cheap gimmick to set you up for a punchline.

At least, I hope you don't lie awake at night wondering what kind of shoes Ninjas wear. If you do, then you need a lot more help than this chapter can provide.

***

Q: Why is your nose in the center of your face?
A: Because it's the scenter of your face.

***

Q: What do you get when you cross a centipede with a parrot?
A: A walkie-talkie.

***

What's the difference between a duck and George Washington? One has a bill on his face, the other, his face on a bill.

***

Q: What's the difference between a well-dressed man on a bicycle and a poorly-dressed man on a unicycle?
A: Attire

***

Q: What do the Movies "Titanic" and "The Sixth Sense" have in common?
A: Icy dead people.

***

Q: What do you call a cubic zirconia in Ireland?
A: A sham-rock

***

Q: What do you call a cow eating grass in your front yard?
A: A lawn-mooer.

***

Q: How does a flea travel?
A: He itch-hikes.

***

Q: What kind of dog doesn't bark?
A: A hush puppy.

***

Q: What did the French chef give his wife for Valentine's Day?
A: A hug and a quiche

***

Q: Which bank does an Orca use?
A; Whales Fargo.

***

Q: Where do snowmen keep their money?

A: In a snow bank.

***

Q: What do you call a cold ghost?
A: Casp-burr!

***

Q: What do women use to stay young looking in the Arctic?
A: Cold cream.

***

Q: How would you describe a chicken staring at a head of Lettuce?
A: Chicken sees a salad.

***

Q So, what is Dr. Pepper's degree in?
A: Fizz-ics

***

Q: What is artificial light made of?
A: Fauxtons

***

Q: How do you describe a cow with one set of legs shorter than the other?
A: Lean beef.

***

Q: What do you call a cow's error?
A: A mis-steak.

***

Q: What do you call a boomerang that does not return to you?
A: A stick.

***

Q: What's a vampire's favorite fruit?
A: necktarines.

***

Q: What's green and sings?
A: Elvis Parsley.

***

Q: Why did the duck say "bang?"
A: Because he was a firequacker.

***

Q: Why do all sheep look alike?
A: Shear coincidence.

***

Q: What do you call a guy with a rubber toe?
A: Roberto.

***

Q: What do sprinters eat before a race?
A; Nothing. They fast.

***

Q: What did the tin man say after he was run over
by a steam roller? A: "Curses, foil again!"

***

Q: What's green and has wheels?
A: Grass. I was wrong about the wheels.

***

Q: Who is a penguin's favorite Aunt?
A: Aunt-Arctica!

***

Q: Why were the middle ages called "dark ages"?
A: There were so many knights.

***

Q: Where should you take someone who has been injured in a peekaboo accident?
A: To the ICU.

***

Q: What's the best way to travel from Norway to Beijing?
A: Oslo boat to China

***

Q: Why don't sharks attack lawyers?
A: Professional courtesy.

***

Q: What goes "oh oh oh"?

A: Santa walking backwards.

***

Q: What do you call a nun walking around aimlessly? A: A Roamin' Catholic.

***

Q: What's the best way to cook alligator?
A: In a croc-pot.

***

Q: Do you know how to make a low IQ person curious?
A: I'll tell you tomorrow.

***

Q: What do you call a sad cup of coffee?
A: Depresso.

***

Q: Why did the Star Wars movies come out in the order 4-5-6 - 1-2-3 ?
A: In charge of the sequence, Yoda was.

***

What has 4 letters, sometimes 9, but never has 5 letters.
Hint: That's not a question.

***

Q: Why can a man never go hungry in a desert?
A: He can eat the sand which is there.

***

Q: How much did Santa pay for his sleigh?
A: Nothing. It was on the house.

***

Q: What do you call a turkey ghost?
A: Poultry-Geist

***

Q: What do you get when you cross a turkey with an octopus?
A: Enough drumsticks for everyone

***

Q: If the pilgrims sailed on the Mayflower, then what did the teachers sail on?

A: Scholar ships.

***

Q: If the Pilgrims were alive today, what would they be most famous for?
A: Being so old!

***

Q: What do you get if you divide the circumference of a pumpkin by its diameter?
A: Pumpkin pi.

***

Q: If April showers bring May flowers, what do May flowers bring?
A: Pilgrims

***

Q: Why can't you take a turkey to church?
A; They use FOWL language.

***

Q: What kind of lights did Noah have on the Ark?
A: Flood lights.

***

Q: How do you make a handkerchief dance?
A: You put a little boogie in it.

***

Q: How does the man on the moon get his haircut?
A: Eclipses it.

***

Q: What do you call a bank officer that rides a horse and wears a black mask?
A: The Loan Arranger.

***

Q: When does a sandwich cook?
A: When it's bakin' lettuce and tomato.

***

Q: What kind of shoes do ninjas wear?
A: Sneakers

***

Q: What do you call a camel with no humps?

A: Humphrey

***

Q: When is a door not a door?
A: When it's ajar.

***

Q: What do you call a statue in a Star Wars gift shop? A: Mannequin Skywalker

***

Q: What do you call a man who has a rubber toe?
A: Roberto

***

Q: Did you hear about the two antennas that got married?
A: The wedding was boring but the reception was excellent.

***

Q: What do you call alphabet soup that only contains the letters M,C,L,V, X and I?
A: Ramen Numerals

***

Q: What's the biggest pan in the world?
A: Japan

***

Q: What's the difference between a politician and a snail?
A: One is slimy, a pest, and leaves a trail everywhere and the other is a snail.

***

Q: What's the difference between a kleptomaniac and a literalist?
A: A literalist takes things literally, and a kleptomaniac takes things, literally.

***

Q: Why do all sheep look alike?
A: Shear coincidence.

***

Q: What did one snowman say to the other snowman? A: "Do you smell carrots?"

***

Q: What's the difference between a golfer and a skydiver?
A: A golfer goes Whack, "damn" and a skydiver goes "damn," whack.

CHAPTER 4

GET OUT THE GROAN-O-METER

Get ready to take a ride, or maybe it would be better to say get ready to be taken for a ride. This chapter is filled with long stories that will end so badly that it'll break your groan-o-meter. But hey, don't they say that most of the fun is the trip to get there?

Buckle your seat belt.

***

Two men were standing inside a building of a local theme park. They were looking outside, and it was an extremely windy day. The area's custodian, the one who had the job of sweeping up debris, was a very small woman who didn't weigh much, and she was having a rough time trying to not be blown away.

One of the men commented to the lady, telling her that she would have to put heavy rocks in her shoes when she went outside to work. The lady looked up and replied, "You mean, now I weigh me down to sweep?"

***

A scientist cloned himself but the experiment created a duplicate who used very foul language. As the clone cursed and swore, the scientist finally pushed it out the window, and it fell to its death.

Later the scientist was arrested for making an obscene clone fall.

***

One morning the family dog was not moving. The mom called the vet who asked her to bring the dog in. After a brief examination, the vet pronounced the dog dead. Are you sure? the distraught woman asked. "He was a great family pet. Isn't there anything else you can do?"

The vet paused for a moment and said, "There is one more thing we can do." He left the room for a moment and came back with a cat and a Labrador retriever. The cat walked over to the dog and eyed the dog from head to toe. The Labrador retriever sniffed the cat thoroughly. Afterwards, both walked sadly from the room.

Well, that confirms it. The vet announced. "Your dog is dead." A bit puzzled, but satisfied that the vet had done everything he possibly could, the woman sighed, "How much do I owe you?" That will be $300. the vet replied. I don't believe it!!!, screamed the woman. "What did you do that cost $300!?

Well, the vet replied, "it's $150 for the cat scan and $150 for the lab test."

***

In the 1900s an English town had fallen on really hard times. For decades its primary industry had been its textile mills, but now the mills were all closed and unemployment was at an all-time high.

Desperate, the town's mayor looked frantically around for other industries to bring to his town.

He found that there was a man in Germany who was looking for someone to take over his thriving hunting dog breeding business. The man had made a fortune raising the animals and was willing to unload it for a fraction of its value, so that he could retire.

The mayor used his influence to have the mills converted to kennels and all of the dogs transported to his town. Employment skyrocketed and the town prospered. Everyone was happy, even though, sometimes--especially on the nights with a full moon--the animals got a little noisy, keeping some residents awake.

But, even these unfortunate few learned to sigh and say, "The mills are alive with the hounds of Munich".

***

I was driving down a lonely northern road one cold winter day when it began to snow pretty heavily. My windows were getting icy and my wiper blades were badly worn and quickly fell apart under the strain.

Unable to drive any further because of the ice building up on my front window I suddenly had a great idea. I stopped and began to overturn large rocks until I located two very lethargic hibernating rattlesnakes. I grabbed them up, straightened them out flat and installed them on my blades, and they worked just fine.

Of course, that's because they were wind-chilled vipers.

***

An elephant and a crocodile were swimming in the Amazon, when the elephant spotted a turtle sunning himself on a rock. The elephant walked over to the turtle, picked him up in his trunk and hurled him far into the jungle. What did you do that for? asked the crocodile. The elephant answered, "That turtle was the one that bit me almost fifty years ago."

The crocodile said, "And you remembered him after all these years? Boy, you sure do have a good memory." Yep, said the elephant. "Turtle recall."

***

A sailor was caught AWOL as he tried to sneak on board his ship at about 3 am. The chief petty officer spied him and ordered the sailor to stop. The officer ordered the sailor, "Take this broom and sweep every link on this anchor chain by morning or it's the brig for you!"

The sailor picked up the broom and started to sweep the chain. Just then, a tern landed on the broom handle. The sailor yelled at the bird to leave, but it didn't. The lad picked the tern off the broom handle, giving the bird a toss. The bird left, only to return and light once again on the broom handle.

The sailor went through the same routine all over again, with the same result. He couldn't get any cleaning done because he could only sweep at the chain once or twice before the silly bird came back.

When morning came, so did the chief petty officer, to check up on his wayward sailor. What on earth have you been doing all night? This chain is no cleaner than when you started! What have you to say for yourself, sailor? barked the chief.

"Honest, chief, 'came the reply, "I tossed a tern all night and couldn't sweep a link!"

***

You probably know that Mahatma Ghandi walked barefoot all the time which developed an impressive set of callouses on both feet. He also ate very little, which made him very frail, and with this odd diet, he suffered from bad breath.

So, this made him a . . . Super-callused fragile mystic hexed by halitosis

***

A young missionary on his first trip to Africa was resting in a clearing when a lion appeared, sauntered over, and sat beside him. As the missionary quietly prayed for deliverance, another lion appeared, slowly walked over and sat on the other side of the missionary.

Considering this a test of his faith, the missionary ever so slowly pulled out his Bible and started reading the gospels. As soon as he started reading, the two lions pounced on him and devoured him.

The moral of the story: Don't try to read between the lions.

***

I am not a fan of toll roads, but on a recent road trip I had no choice. There was a huge back up on one tollway as a car had just rammed a toll booth and smashed the gate.

As we waited in the traffic jam, the car was towed, and as the traffic started inching forward again, we saw a repair truck pull up to the damaged toll booth. In the short time that traffic cleared and we reached the toll gates, the damaged gate and booth were already repaired, and working again! I couldn't help but remark to the toll attendant about how amazingly fast they had made the repairs.

She said yes, it was because they had used toll gate booth paste.

***

NASA announced plans to put a number of cows in orbit to test the effect it will have on milk production.

They're going to call it "the herd shot 'round the world."

***

The church was badly in need of a coat of paint. So, the pastor decided he'd do the job himself.

But all he had was one bucket of paint. So, he thinned the one bucket of paint enough to cover the entire church. Then he spent all day painting.

That night it rained—very hard—and washed all the paint off.

The pastor was quite discouraged and asked God, 'Why...why God, did you let it rain and wash off all my hard work?'

To which God thundered his reply, 'Repaint! Repaint! And thin no more!'

***

A friend lived in New Orleans and commissioned an artist friend, Hugh, to paint a portrait of his girlfriend.

When it was done his girlfriend called to tell him to pick it up and pay Hugh for it.

She gave him the directions as: "Drive past my house, and his studio is down by the water."

As he hung up he said "I'll go by you to buy you, by Hugh, at the bayou...Bye, you!"

***

Apparently, it's no longer politically correct to direct a joke at any racial or ethnic minority so.......

An Englishman, a Scotsman, an Irishman, a Welshman, a Latvian, a Turk, an Australian, a Kiwi, an Indonesian, an American, a German, a Peruvian, an Egyptian, a Japanese, a Mexican, a Spaniard, a Russian, a Pole, a Lithuanian, a Tibetan, a Swede, a Finn, an Israeli, a Romanian, a Bulgarian, a Serb, a Swiss, a Greek, a Singaporean, a Kazhak, an Italian, a Norwegian, a Dane, a Ugandan, a Nigerian, a Frenchman, a Colombian, an Argentinian and a South African went to a night club.

The bouncer said: "Sorry, I can't let you in without a Thai."

***

Elvis Costello and Abba are planning a tour concert this summer. But they can't determine in which order they'll appear each night.

So, I guess we will have to watch Abba and Costello to find out who's on first.

***

I'm starting a new restaurant. The featured menu item will be a baked potato, loose on a plate, covered with curry, followed by a serving of peas.

I'm calling it: "Curry on my wayward spud. There'll be peas when you are done."

***

Did you ever wonder why there are no dead penguins on the ice in Antarctica? Where do they all go?

The penguin is a very ritualistic bird and lives an extremely ordered and complex life. Penguins mate for life, as well as maintain a form of compassionate contact with their offspring throughout their life.

If a penguin is found dead, members of the family and social circle dig holes in the ice, using only their vestigial wings and beaks, until the hole is deep enough for the dead bird to be rolled into, and buried.   After packing the ice back in the hole, the male penguins then gather in a circle around the fresh grave and sing: "Freeze a jolly good fellow. Freeze a jolly good fellow."

You really didn't believe that I know anything about penguins, did you?

***

I needed to repair a leaking toilet, so I researched toilet flappers. The Internet is a treasure trove of information, sometimes historical.

Little did I know that in the old days, toilet flappers were once made from the skin of a small animal, whose skin would perform superbly when it was cut to the shape needed to perform as a toilet flapper. Hardy hunters would go into the forest to set traps and collect the valuable animals.

As with most things in life, people compete, but in this case, the hunters would compete, not for who caught how much, but, in this case, who was the best dressed hunter. After the best-dressed competition, the hunters would be sent off by a personal encourager, and there was thunderous applause from a gathered crowd as the hunters took off on their trek for the elusive creatures.

The story takes on one additional level of peculiarity because all these events originated in the edge of the forest, where there were often no roads. As a result, someone would have to create and distribute a unique map each year so that the hunters and their encouragers could assemble at the starting point.

So, the map creator became an indispensable and semi-famous person in the region. This person, the final one in the process, became known as . . . Get ready . . . Wait for it . . .The Dapper crapper flapper trapper clapper mapper.

***

In case you missed it . . . There's a new restaurant that has an unusual choice for the pre-entree selections. You can choose either broth with rice, or you can opt for an anti-social waiter named Rex, working on his degree who will perform lame magic tricks while he delivers a salad, but in several small servings.

The menu lists this as: "Soup or college magic misfit Rex with salad doses."

***

There's a new brightly colored, but cheap lipstick brand on the market. They tried to get Julie Andrews as a spokesperson. She tried it, but refused to endorse it. She Said . . . "The super color fragile lipstick gives me halitosis."

***

Not too long ago, a ship spotted a desert island with a single stranded survivor living on it.

Upon landing, to rescue him, the captain notices that there are three huts. Asking about the first, the man replied: "That's my house." The captain asked about the second hut, and the man replies: "That's my church." "And the third", the captain asked?

 The man answers: "That's the church I used to go to."

***

Tired of constantly being broke and stuck in an unhappy marriage, a young husband decided to solve both problems by taking out a large insurance policy on his wife with himself as the beneficiary and then arranging to have her killed.

A 'friend of a friend' put him in touch with a nefarious dark-side underworld figure who went by the name of 'Artie.' Artie explained to the husband that his going price for snuffing out a spouse was $10,000. The Husband said he was willing to pay that amount but that he wouldn't have any cash on hand until he could collect his wife's insurance money. Artie insisted on being paid at least something up front, so the man opened his wallet, displaying the single dollar bill that rested inside. Artie sighed, rolled his eyes and reluctantly agreed to accept the dollar as down payment for the dirty deed.

A few days later, Artie followed the man's wife to the local Costco Supermarket. There, he surprised her in the produce department and proceeded to attempt to strangle her with his gloved hands. As the poor unsuspecting woman struggled and started to slump to the floor, the manager of the produce department stumbled unexpectedly onto the scene.

Unwilling to leave any living witnesses behind, ol' Artie had no choice but to try to strangle the produce manager as well. However, unknown to Artie, the entire proceedings were captured by the hidden security cameras and observed by the shop's security guard, who immediately called the police.

Artie was caught and arrested before he could even leave the premises. Under intense questioning at the police station, Artie revealed the whole sordid plan, including his unusual financial arrangements with the hapless husband who was also quickly arrested.

The next day in the newspaper, the headline declared... "Artie Chokes 2 for $1 @ Costco"

***

A kindergarten teacher gave her class a "show and tell" assignment. Each student was instructed to bring in an object that represented their religion to share with the class.

The first student got up in front of the class and said, "My name is Benjamin and I am Jewish and this is a Star of David."

The second student got up in front of the class and said, "My name is Mary. I'm a Catholic and this is a Rosary."

The third student got in up front of the class and said, "My name is Tommy. I am Baptist and this is a casserole."

***

It was a hot summer's day, and Luke was in the marina, having a few beers aboard his boat, patriotically named the "Fourth of July." He was waiting for his friend, Opie, to arrive so they could go for a cruise. Opie was late, unfortunately, because he had to pick up his wife from her appointment with the obstetrician.

Her examinations were cheap because the doctor, a fellow named Juan, was Opie's cousin. Anyway, the appointment went overtime, and Opie was late getting to the marina. Luke had been drinking all this time, and was feeling no pain.

When he saw Opie finally walking down the pier, he jumped up, staggered to the side of the boat to wave to his friend, and nearly fell in! Opie got there just in time to grab Luke.

Thus, it was that O. B. Juan's kin, Opie, saved Luke from falling to the dock side of the Fourth.

***

A skeptical anthropologist was cataloging South American folk remedies with the assistance of a tribal medicine man who indicated that the leaves of a particular fern were a sure cure for any case of constipation.

When the anthropologist expressed his doubts, the medicine man looked him in the eye and said, "Let me tell you, with fronds like these, you don't need enemas."

***

Back in the 1800's the Tate's Watch Company of Massachusetts wanted to produce other products, and since they already made the cases for watches, they used them to produce compasses.

The new compasses were so bad that people often ended up in Canada or Mexico rather than California.

This, of course, is the origin of the expression -- "He who has a Tate's is lost!"

***

King Ozymandias of Assyria was running low on cash after years of war with the Hittites. His last great possession was the Star of the Euphrates, the most valuable diamond in the ancient world.

Desperate, he went to Croesus, the pawnbroker, to ask for a loan. Croesus said, "I'll give you 100,000 dinars for it." "But I paid a million dinars for it," the King protested. "Don't you know who I am? I am the king!"

Croesus replied, "When you wish to pawn a Star, makes no difference who you are."

***

One sunny day, a frog walked into the bank and headed straight to the first teller he saw. Her name was Ms. Paddywhack. In a sad voice, the frog explained that he's hit upon some sad times and he needs a $50,000 loan to get through it all.

"Do you have any collateral?", asks Ms. Paddywhack. I have this little keychain with a little pink elephant... says the frog. Oh...how about any references? The frog produces some paperwork to the effect that he's actually Mick Jagger's son.

Ms. Paddywhack, utterly confused, goes into the back room and explains the situation to her manager. "There's a frog outside asking for a $50,000 loan, and he says he's Mick Jagger's son, and all he has is this awful ... I don't even know what this is!"

After reviewing the situation, the manager calmly says: it's a knick-knack, Paddywhack! Give the frog a loan. His old man's a Rolling Stone!"

***

I was in the restaurant/bar of a resort island recently. Because everything has to come by ferry (it's an island), the bar has just one featured beer on draft each day.

Because the beer they serve is strong, I was slowly nursing a schooner until the ferry arrived to take me back to the mainland. At the scheduled time, the ferry sounds a horn alerting would-be passengers of departure in 5 minutes.

As I was waiting for the 5-minute warning horn for the ferry's leaving, I heard the extended clanging of a bell. Looking over to the dock I saw the Skipper of the ferry banging on the ship's bell.

I later learned that the Ship's horn was broken. So, there I was . . . sitting on the bock of the day, watching the ride toll away.

***

A tourist in Vienna was walking through a graveyard and all of a sudden he heard music. No one was around, so he started searching for the source. He finally located the origin and found it was coming from a grave with a headstone that reads: "Ludwig van Beethoven, 1770- 1827".

Then he realizes that the music was Beethoven's Ninth Symphony and it was being played backward! Puzzled, he left the graveyard and persuaded a friend to return with him.

By the time they arrived back at the grave, the music had changed. This time it was the Seventh Symphony, but like the previous piece, it was being played backwards. Curious, the men agreed to consult a music scholar.

When they returned with the expert, the Fifth Symphony was playing, again backwards. The expert noticed that the symphonies were being played in the reverse order in which they were composed, the 9th, then the 7th, then the 5th.

By the next day the word had spread, and a crowd had gathered around the grave. They were all listening to the Second Symphony being played backward.

Just then the graveyard's caretaker ambled up to the group. Someone in the group asked him if he had an explanation for the music.

"I would have thought it was obvious," the caretaker said. "He's decomposing."

***

Mary Poppins, when she retired from the nanny business, opened a roadside stand on the west coast. Her service was predicting when people would get bad breath.

Can you guess what the sign on the front of her stand said?

"Super California Mystic, Expert: Halitosis"

***

Ollie Oyster and Sam Clam were best friends. They grew up together, went to school together, and even played in a rock band together.

One day they had a horrible car accident, and both died. Ollie had lived a good life, and went to heaven. Sam went to the other place. Ollie wanted to play in a rock band again, just like before he died. But the only instrument allowed in heaven was the harp. He was a little sad about it, but learned to play the harp anyway, and became pretty good at it.

But Ollie Oyster missed his good friend Sam Clam. One day he asked God if he could visit Sam. God said "Well, we don't normally do that kind of thing.

But you were a very good oyster, so I can make a small exception. I'll let you visit Sam for one day. But the catch is, you have to take your harp with you. They don't have harps in hell, so when you want to get back into heaven just come to the front gate and play your harp, and we'll know it's you and let you in."

Ollie was overjoyed, grabbed his harp, and went to visit his old friend. Ollie found Sam, and they soon caught up on old times. Musical instruments of many kinds were allowed in hell, and Sam had formed a band, made a lot of money, and eventually opened his own disco. The two friends partied the night away in Sam's disco, talking about old times, drinking heavily, and having a great time.

Finally, Ollie realized that time had gotten away from him, and he had only minutes to get back to heaven. He rushed out of the disco, leaving his harp behind. He made it to the front gates of heaven, and pounded on the door. St Peter peeked out, and said "God told me you would be coming back, but I can't let you in until I hear you play your harp!"

Ollie cried "Oh No! I left my harp in Sam Clam's disco!"

***

An obscure tribe on a South Pacific island had the unusual practice of electing a new king every 10 years.

One of the perks of being king was custody of a beautiful, mahogany, jewel-studded throne. The throne was spectacular in appearance and comfort. As one particular King's reign was coming to an end, he became more and more agitated about losing the throne. Not only would he have to move out of the beautiful palace and back into his grass hut, but he would forever lose access to that beautiful throne!

The night before the new King was to take office, the outgoing King had his palace staff remove the throne and hide it in the bamboo rafters of his hut.

Unfortunately, the throne was too heavy for the rafters. One night, the throne broke through the rafters, crashing down on the King's bed and killing him instantly.

The moral of the story? People who live in grass houses shouldn't stow thrones.

***

After Quasimodo's death, the bishop of the cathedral of Notre Dame sent word through the streets of Paris that a new bell ringer was needed. The bishop decided that he would conduct the interviews personally and went up into the belfry to begin the screening process.

After observing several applicants demonstrate their skills, he was about to call it a day when a lone, armless man approached him and announced that he was there to apply for the bell ringer's job. The bishop was incredulous, "You have no arms!" No matter, said the man, "Observe!"

He then began striking the bells with his face, producing a beautiful melody on the carillon. The bishop listened in astonishment, convinced that he had finally found a suitable replacement for Quasimodo.

Suddenly, when rushing forward to strike a bell, the armless man tripped, and plunged headlong out of the belfry window to his death in the street below. The stunned bishop rushed to his side. When he reached the street, a crowd had gathered around the fallen figure, drawn by the beautiful music they had heard only moments before.

As they silently parted to let the bishop through, one of them asked, "Bishop, who was this man?" I don't know his name, the bishop sadly replied, "but his face rings a bell."

***

(but wait, there's more...)

The following day, despite the sadness that weighed heavily on his heart due to the unfortunate death of the armless campanologist, the bishop continued his interviews for the bell ringer of Notre Dame.

The first man to approach him said, "Your excellency, I am the brother of the poor, armless wretch that fell to his death from this very belfry yesterday. I pray that you honor his life by allowing me to replace him in this duty." The bishop agreed to give the man an audition, and as the armless man's brother stooped to pick up a mallet to strike the first bell, he groaned, clutched at his chest and died on the spot.

Two monks, hearing the bishop's cries of grief at this second tragedy, rushed up the stairs to his side. What has happened? the first breathlessly asked, "Who is this man?"

"I don't know his name," sighed the distraught bishop, "but he's a dead ringer for his brother.

Linoleum Blownapart

***

CHAPTER 5

I THOUGHT GROWING OLD WOULD TAKE LONGER

What was I going to write here? I don't remember. Oh well, read these, and if you're old you'll recognize yourself. If you're not, now you'll have something to . . . er . . . look forward to.

***

As I get older and think about all the people I've lost along the way, I think . . . maybe a career as a tour guide wasn't for me.

***

You know you're getting old when clothes you used to wear are now someone's Halloween costume.

***

I have entered the snapdragon part of life. Part of me has snapped, and the rest is draggin'

***

I have so many aches and pains that I think I have that Chinese disease: "Yung No Mo."

***

If I am ever on life support and not responding, try unplugging and plugging me back in. See if that works.

***

Going to bed early. Not leaving the house. Taking a nap. What were once my childhood punishments are now my daily goals.

***

These days, I spend a lot of time thinking about the hereafter. I go somewhere to get something, and then when I get there, I wonder what I'm here after.

***

I have decided to retire and live off of my savings. Not sure what I'll do the week after that.

***

I was trying to remember that group I liked in the 70s. The best I could come up with was "Carrying Grain." Turns out it was Hall & Oates.

***

My grandson was born today. In the hospital, another grandpa congratulated me, and said that his granddaughter was born yesterday. "who knows" he said. "Maybe someday they'll get married."

Sure, like my grandson is going to marry someone twice his age.

***

My career has been an interesting path.

My best job was a Musician, but I eventually found I wasn't noteworthy.

Next, I attempted being a Deli Worker, but any way I sliced it.... I couldn't cut the mustard.

I studied a long time to become a Doctor, but didn't have any patience.

Next, was a job in a Shoe Factory. Tried hard but just didn't fit in. I only worked there for one sole month.

I became a Professional Fisherman. I was hooked on the job, but discovered I couldn't live on my net income.

Then I managed to get a good job working for a Pool Maintenance Company, but the work was just too draining. And they caught me skimming the profits.

So, then I got a job in a Workout Center, but they said I wasn't fit for the job.

After many years of trying to find steady work, I finally got a job as a Historian - but there was no future in it.

My last job was working in Starbucks, but I had to quit because it was the same old grind.

SO, I TRIED RETIREMENT AND I FOUND I'M PERFECT FOR THE JOB!

***

You know you're getting older when you realize that caution is the only thing you care to exercise.

***

You know you're getting old when it takes longer to rest than it did to get tired.

***

You know you're getting old when you're sitting in a rocker and you can't get it started.

***

It's hard to be nostalgic when you can't remember anything.

***

You know you're getting old when you wake up with that morning-after feeling, and you didn't do anything the night before.

***

Yesterday, it was so windy that I had to wrinkle my forehead and screw my cap on to keep it from flying off.

***

Ironic thought: When we were young, we would sneak out of our house to go to parties. Now, we sneak out of parties to go home.

***

<u>1980 vs. 2020:</u>

1980 - long hair;   2020 - longing for hair
1980 - Keg;   2020 - EKG
1980 - Acid rock;   2020 - acid reflux
1980 - Going to a new, hip joint;
                             2020 - getting a new hip
joint
1980 - Rolling Stones;   2020 - kidney stones
1980 - Disco;   2020 - Costco

Chapter 6

PENGUINS TO PANCAKES

All kinds of stuff in this chapter, some of it is even kinda funny. Actually, most of it is downright entertaining.

***

Two penguins were on an ice floe.
One turned to the other and said, "You look like you're wearing a tuxedo."
The other responded, "What makes you think I'm not?"

***

***

Geology rocks, but geography is where it's at.

***

I used to think I was indecisive. Now, I'm not so sure.

***

If the person who named the walkie talkie named other things . . .

- Stamps: Lickie Stickie
- Defibrillators: Hearty Starty
- Bumble Bees: Fuzzy Buzzy
- Pregnancy Test: Maybe Baby
- Fork: Stabby Grabby
- Socks: Feety Heaty
- Hippo: Floatie Bloatie
- Nightmare: Screamy Dreamy
- Dessert: Sweetie Treatie

***

If we added Puerto Rico, DC and Guam, we'd have 53 states. 53 is a prime number. Then we'd really be one nation, indivisible.

***

If I make you breakfast in bed, a simple "thank you" will suffice. None of this "How did you get into my house?" business.

***

I walked into a toy store to do some Christmas shopping and asked the clerk, "Where are the Schwarzenegger dolls? "
He said: "Aisle B, back."

***

UPS: Your package is in Houston, on a truck driven by Bob and will be delivered at 2:30 PM today.
FedEx: Your package is coming, and you'll get it when we give it to you.
Amazon: We're inside your house.
Facebook: We know you've been thinking about a new toaster, and here are 15 toaster ads for the next 15 days.
USPS: You ordered something?

***

Just a thought . . . there hasn't been a bacon recall in years, but there have been several vegetable recalls.

***

My mother told me that I was different . . . . . . but from now on, I'm going to be the same.

***

This morning, I thought my Alpha-Bits were haunted because all they spelled was: "Ooooooo." Then my wife told me I was eating Cheerios.

***

Apparently, there is a bipartisan push in the US Senate to legalize marijuana for arthritis treatment. So, in other words, there's joint support for joint support for joint support.

***

I got in a good round of golf yesterday. I was three over. One over a house, one over a patio, and one over a swimming pool.

***

Everyone laughed when I told them I'd be a great standup comedian. Well, they're not laughing now!

***

I just found out that I'm color blind. The news came completely out of the green!

***

It's gonna be a rough day. Last night I dreamed that I was a muffler. I woke up exhausted.

***

Knock, knock. Who's there? I'm a pile up . . .

***

Heard in class: Teacher: "Timmy, please use the word gruesome in a sentence." Timmy: "I used to be shorter, but then I grew some."

***

One day, in my Catholic school cafeteria, a nun put a note in front of the pile of apples, " Take only one. God is watching." Further down the line were the cookies. Someone else made another note, "Take as many as you want. God is watching the apples."

***

I want to be more self-sufficient, and to start growing my own food. Does anyone know where I can get bacon seeds?

***

There are just too many imports. I just bought a new TV and it has a label on the back that read: "Built-in Antenna." I don't even know where that is.

***

I went to the store to buy two copies of "Math for Dummies" at $11.99 each. The smart-alec clerk tried to charge me $50.

***

A friend sent me a "get better soon" card. I'm not sick. Do you think he's trying to tell me something?

***

Whenever it rains, my kids just stand at the window, looking kinda sad. Maybe I should let them in.

***

My friend tells me that I'm too skeptical. But, I don't believe a word he says.

***

I'm reading a horror story in Braille. Something bad is going to happen, I can feel it

***

Have you noticed how many people today just write "Congrats"?
They must not know how to spell congradjulashions.

***

Auto-correct makes me say things I didn't nintendo.

***

What I if told you . . .
You just read that line wrong?

***

"To do is to be" - Nietzsche.
"To be is to do" - Kant.
"Do be do be do" - Sinatra.

***

So, there's a lot of fuss about 3D printers that can print guns. I'm not impressed. I've had a Canon printer for years.

***

My mischievous friend wants to be a judge in a spelling bee. He wants to ask the contestants to spell the word "there." When they ask for it to be used in a sentence, he'll say: "Their car is parked over there, because they're late."

***

Yesterday, I found a book titled: "How to solve half of your problems in just days." So, I bought two.

***

I'm writing my autobiography. But, for the life of me, I can't think of a title.

***

I ordered a chicken and an egg from Amazon. I'll let you know . . .

***

Got a job overseeing MacDonald's farm. I'm the new CIEIO.

***

It's been really busy here at the clock repair shop. I can't tell you how long I've been here.

***

Counselor: How many introverts does it take to change a light bulb? Client: Does it have to be a group activity?

***

I have a fear of speed bumps . . . but I'm slowly getting over it.

***

My poor knowledge of Greek mythology has always been my Achilles elbow.

***

There's a rumor that YouTube, Twitter, and Facebook may merge. They're thinking of naming the combined company: "You-Twit-Face."

***

When I was a child, my mother fed me alphabet soup. She told me I would love it. She was just putting words in my mouth.

***

Have you ever tried blindfolded target practice? You don't know what you're missing.

***

My friend the drummer had twin daughters. Know what he named them?   Anna one, Anna two . . .

***

I want to grow seedless watermelons but I can't find the seeds.

***

Interviewing for a job the other day, I answered one of the questions: "The sky's the limit." I didn't get the job. I guess that wasn't a good answer when interviewing at NASA.

***

I can't see an end. I have no control. There's no escape. And I don't have a home anymore. I think it's time for a new keyboard.

***

Would you like to join . . .
- The Yoko club? O, no.
- The compulsive rhymers club? Okey, dokey.
- The German philosophy club? I Kant.
- The Codependency club? Can I bring a friend?
- The procrastinators club? Maybe next week.

***

I hate people who use big words just to make themselves look perspicacious.

***

I shut down my ice sculpture business. Liquidated it.

***

Never criticize someone until you've walked a mile in their shoes. That way, when you criticize them, they won't be able to hear you from that far away. And you'll have their shoes.

***

I was going to post a time travel pun. But nobody liked it.

***

I just wrote a book on reverse psychology. Don't buy it.

***

I am looking to find a new home for a small dog. He is a terrier and he barks a lot. If you are interested, just let me know, and I'll climb into the neighbor's yard and get him for you.

***

Today, I was mugged by an invisible man. Boy, I did not see that coming.

***

My therapist told me: "Write letters to the people you hate, and then burn them." Did that. Now what do I do with the letters?

***

I'm more than mad at myself that I forgot what 51, 6 and 500 are in Roman Numerals. I'm LIVID.

***

I tried to read a book today on the history of Scotch Tape . . . but I couldn't find the beginning.

***

I went to a crime writer's dinner once. Everyone was afraid to taste the soup.

***

I was pulled over by a police officer. He asked if I had a Police record. Apparently "Roxanne" wasn't the answer he wanted to hear.

***

I ordered a pizza last night. Was asked if I wanted it cut into six slices or eight. I thought about it and replied: "I'm watching my weight, cut it into six."

***

I bought the new book "CPR For Dummies" only to find out that it was for ventriloquists.

***

I just bought a Thesaurus and came home to find that all the pages are blank. I have no words to describe how angry I am.

***

I hear the French don't like fast food. I guess that's why they eat snails.

***

Yesterday I went to a temporary tattoo parlor to get a tattoo. This morning it wouldn't wash off. So, I went back to complain. The tattoo parlor wasn't there.

***

It is said that people in Dubai do not understand the humor of the Flintstones. But I know for a fact that the people in Abu Dhabi do.

***

If asked to use one word to describe myself, it would be" "Not good at following directions."

***

I signed up for a mime class. There's no telling what I'll learn.

***

My friend says that Comforters are always superior to Quilts on a bed. I don't think he should be making blanket statements.

***

I am going to try to be a minimalist. It's the least I can do.

***

Overheard: "Yeah, I can pretty much never sit by the pool anymore." - MARCO POLO

***

Every year, hundreds of students enroll in mime school . . . never to be heard from again.

***

Last week it was so cold that Starbucks was serving coffee on a stick!

***

 Last week it was so cold that we had to chop up the piano for firewood (but we only got two chords.)

***

Last week it was so cold that words froze in the air. To hear what someone said, we had to take them in and warm them by the fire!

***

Last week it was so cold that when we milked the cows today, we got ice cream.

***

Last week it was so cold that I chipped a tooth on my soup.

***

I read today that if I weigh 250 lbs. on earth, I'd weigh 95 lbs. on Mars. I'm not overweight. I'm just on the wrong planet.

***

I had a very productive day today. I was able to accomplish much more procrastinating than I had planned.

***

I'm going to start selling blank bumper stickers for people who don't want to get involved.

***

You know what I find really odd? Numbers not divisible by two.

***

I'm going to start a movement called "All sleep matters."

***

I, for one, like Roman numerals.

***

There's a photographer who went completely insane trying to take a close-up photo of the horizon.

***

I've learned two very important lessons in my life. The first, I can't remember. And the second is that I need to start writing things down.

***

One of my New Years' resolutions is to make the little things count . . . so I'm going to start teaching math to babies.

***

The right shoes for the right people . . .

- Artists – skechers

- Burglars – sneakers
- Pilots – wing tips
- Professors – oxfords
- Physicians – doc martens
- Bankers – cashews
- Clumsy people – slippers
- Politicians – flip flops

***

I was feeling insignificant in this world the other day, but then I was reminded that I am unique, just like everyone else.

***

I love the way the earth rotates. It makes my day.

***

I read today that a new study shows that humans eat more bananas than monkeys. That makes sense. I can't remember the last time I ate a monkey.

***

A recent study shows that exaggerations went up by a million percent last year.

***

My friend the poor speller wrote that he wants his firstborn to be a mail child. I told him to keep us posted.

***

Yesterday, after an appointment, I asked the receptionist to validate my parking.
She said: "You did a great job. Evenly spaced, and at nearly a perfect right angle."

***

I'm trying to come up with a joke about infinity. But it doesn't have an ending.

***

Green is my favorite color. I like it better than blue and yellow combined.

***

What do you get when you cross a four-leaf clover with poison ivy? A rash of good luck.

***

What's Irish and stays outside all year? Patty O'Furniture.

***

An oxymoron walked into a bar . . . The silence was deafening.

***

Yesterday, I had an overwhelming feeling that everything was coming my way. As it turned out, I was on the wrong side of the road.

***

I'm really good at pantomimes . . . even if I can't say so myself.

***

This morning I put instant coffee in a microwave oven and almost went back in time.

***

Me: OMG, there's a wolf.
Wife: Where?

Me: No, the regular kind.

***

I'm giving up autocorrect for Lint.

***

My boss says I have only two faults: one, I don't listen, and some other stuff he kept rattling on about.

***

Do you ever wake up, kiss the person sleeping beside you, and feel glad that you are alive? I have a friend who did that, and now he can't fly on that airline any more.

***

What's your secret super power? Mine is meeting people, then instantly forgetting their names.

***

I hate being bipolar. It's awesome.

***

Yesterday in Starbucks, I gave my name as "The Lord be with you." When the barista shouted my name, half the customers shouted: "and with your spirit." and the other half shouted: "and also with you."
It was a right ecumenical mess.

***

The difference between a Harley and a Hoover?
Location of the dirtbag.

***

Her: Have you heard of Murphy's law?
Me: No, what is it?
Her: If something can go wrong, it will.
Me: Okay, have you heard of Cole's law?
Her: No, what is it?
Me: Thinly sliced cabbage.

***

Overheard in a local pub:
Bartender: "What'll you have?"
Skeleton: "I'll have a beer and a mop."

***

As a child, my mother told me I could be anyone I wanted to be... Turns out the police refers to this as "Identity Fraud"

***

My uncle used to tell me: "Don't be too quick to find faults." He was a good man . . . but a terrible geologist.

***

I'm going to write a science fiction novel about a parallel universe where people constantly wonder where all the extra socks come from.

***

If I had 50 cents for every math test I ever failed, I'd have $6.30 by now.

***

The three unwritten rules of business:
1.
2.
3.

***

I come from a family of failed magicians. I have two half-sisters.

***

Someone said that if you hold a Shell up you can hear the sea. My friend tried that, and got six years for armed robbery.

***

Plagiarism - getting in trouble for something you didn't do.

***

Funny, I don't remember being absent minded.

***

Funny, I don't remember being absent minded.

***

If you want your children to listen to you, try talking softly to someone else.

***

I know a guy who is so obnoxious he can brighten up a room just by walking out of it.

***

For the last couple of years, I've been getting most of my clothes online. Unfortunately, the neighbors have started taking their washing in at night.

***

I recently read "Great Expectations." It wasn't as good as I thought it would be.

***

I bought a sweater, but had to take it back because it kept picking up so much static electricity. They gave me another . . . free of charge.

***

Congratulations to Quaker Oats for their decisive move on renaming their Aunt Jemima pancake mix. Under the circumstances, I would have expected them to . . . waffle.

***

I have a Fibonacci joke, and it's as bad as the last two you heard combined.

***

I'm thinking of opening a new restaurant called Karma. There'll be no menu; everyone will get what they deserve.

***

Being Polish has many challenges. I went to an appointment with the eye doctor. As part of the testing of my eyes, the nurse held up a card with the letters: CZWIXNSSTACZ. She asked if I could read it. "Read it?" I replied. "I know him."

***

The patron saint of copying people on email is St. Francis of a CC.

***

I saw an ad for cemetery plots, and I thought to myself: "This is the last thing I need."

***

Overheard from two adjacent stalls in a men's room:
"Hey buddy, I seem to be out of toilet paper. Can you spare some?"
"Sorry, I'm all out."
"Then, do you have any Kleenex?"
"Sorry, no,"
. . Pause . . .
"Do you have change for a ten?"

***

When I was younger, my girlfriend said she was leaving me because I kept pretending to be a Transformer. I told her: "No, wait! I can change."

***

I'm giving up eating chocolate for a month. Sorry, bad punctuation. I'm giving up; eating chocolate for a month.

***

I just melted an ice cube with my mind by staring at it. It took a lot longer than I thought it would.

***

After years of wanting to fix things around the house but lacking the time, this week I discovered that wasn't the reason.

***

Books I am reading:

> Crime & Punishment USA, by Penny Tentiary
> DIY Bricklaying, by Bill Jerome Wall
> Before Digital, by Anna Logg
> The Lion Attacked, by Claude Yurarrmov;
> Olympic Trials, by Willy Qualify.
> Heart Surgery in Ireland, by Angie O'Plasty;
> Crossed The Dessert, by Rhoda Camel.

***

The bartender says: "We don't serve time travelers in here." A time traveler walks into a bar.

***

So, after winning a game, I threw the ball into the crowd, like I see them do on TV. Apparently, that's not acceptable in bowling.

***

I will always be disappointed that a group of squids is not called a squad.

***

I have a friend who is so lazy he puts popcorn in his pancakes so they will turn over by themselves

CHAPTER 7

BECOME A SUCCESSFUL BOUILLONAIRE

A collection of observations, advice and tips on how to better navigate life. And if you're getting your life advice from a book like this, you may need more help than this chapter can provide.

***

If at first you don't succeed . . . then maybe skydiving isn't for you.

***

***

I think the laziest person of all time may be the guy who named the fireplace.

***

If life hands you a melon . . . you might be dyslexic.

***

If someone asks you to spell part backwards, don't do it. It's a trap.

***

A boiled egg is hard to beat.

***

Remember, there's just a fine line between numerator and denominator.

***

If you're buying one of those Smart Water products for $4 a bottle, it's not working.

***

***

Cosmetic surgery used to be such a taboo subject. Now you can talk about Botox and nobody raises an eyebrow.

***

Technically, Moses was the first person with a tablet downloading data from the cloud.

***

A fine is a tax for doing wrong. A tax is a fine for doing well.

***

Research shows that the average human body contains enough bones to make an entire skeleton.

***

Do not touch must be one of the scariest things to read in Braille

***

Never trust someone with graph paper. They're always plotting something.

***

Socialist jokes aren't funny . . . . . . unless everyone gets them.

***

My bed is a magical place where I can suddenly remember everything I was supposed to do.

***

The easiest way to find something you've been looking for is to buy a replacement.

***

The good thing about lending someone your time machine is that you basically get it back immediately.

***

Never in the history of calm down has anyone calmed down by being told to calm down.

***

Facial recognition software can pick a person out of a crowd of thousands, but the vending machine at work can't recognize a dollar bill with a bent corner.

***

Dyslexics are teople poo.

***

Age is strictly a case of mind over matter. If you don't mind, it doesn't matter.

***

Most people love working from home . . . except firefighters.

***

He who comes forth with a fifth on the fourth may not come forth on the fifth.

***

Some cause happiness wherever they go. Others whenever they go.

***

Red, white and blue are the true colors of freedom.
Unless they are flashing from the car behind you.

***

Whoever said "ought of sight, out of mind" never
had a big spider disappear under their bed.

***

If you look really closely, all mirrors look like
eyeballs.

***

Outside of a dog, a book is man's best friend. Inside
of a dog, it's too dark to read.

***

There are three types of people in the world. Those
who can count and those that can't.

***

An apple a day . . . . . . will keep anyone away, if
thrown hard enough.

***

It must take a giraffe forever to puke.

***

Just a warning if you're buying a watch on Amazon. If it says you can swim with it, this only applies if you can swim without it.

***

Never put off till tomorrow what may be done day after tomorrow just as well.

***

Some people should use a glue stick instead of chapstick.

***

Light travels faster than sound. That's why some people appear bright until you hear them speak.

***

Good judgement is a product of Wisdom.

Wisdom is a product of experience.
Experience is a product of . . . poor judgement.

***

Organized people are simply too lazy to search for stuff.

***

Make sure to bring up politics at Thanksgiving dinner this year. It's a way to save on Christmas gifts.

***

The fastest land mammal is a toddler who's been asked what's in their mouth.

***

Courage is knowing it might hurt, and doing it anyway. Stupidity is the same. And, that's why life is hard.

***

It seems like the world only beats a path to my door when I'm in the bathroom.

***

I'm investing in stocks. Beef, chicken and vegetable. Someday, I hope to be a bouillonaire.

Linoleum Blownapart

CHAPTER 8

THERE ARE VEGANS OUT THERE NAMED HUNTER

You may need to see a doctor after this chapter. Some of these diet, health and fitness remarks may give you nausea.

***

Doctor: You're overweight, and need to go on a diet.
Patient: For that I definitely want a second opinion.
Doctor: Okay, you're ugly, too.

***

Getting fat wasn't my intention. It was a pure and clear snaccident.

***

Overheard in my doctor's office:
"Doctor, there's a patient on line one that says he's invisible."
"Well, tell him I can't see him right now."

***

I ate a box of Thin Mints. Didn't get any thinner. I don't think they work.

***

Here's a thought for the day: There are vegans out there named Hunter.

***

I stepped on my scale this morning. The readout said: "Please use social distancing. One person at a time."

***

I just got over my addiction to chocolate, marshmallows and nuts. I won't lie. It was a rocky road.

***

I've been doing crunches twice a day.   Captain in the morning. Nestle in the afternoon.

***

I thought I saw an eye doctor on an Alaskan island, but it was just an optical Aleutian.

***

Yesterday I accidentally swallowed some food coloring. The doctor says I'm okay, but I feel like I've dyed a little inside.

***

Whenever I try to eat healthy, a chocolate bar looks at me and snickers.

***

My brain cells, hair cells, and skin cells continue to die. But, my fat cells seem to have eternal life.

***

It's rare when a defibrillator fails to work. But when it happens, no one is shocked.

***

I had my annual checkup today at the doctor. He told me my sugar level was too high. So, I promptly came home, went to my kitchen, and moved it to a lower shelf.

***

Before my surgery the anesthetist offered to knock me out with gas or a boat paddle. It was an ether/oar situation

***

My Doctor: "I'm prescribing you a drug that can help you with your insomnia problem."
Me: "Great, how often do I have to take it?"
My Doctor: "Every two hours."

***

Two friends were considering brain transplants. One went through with it and one didn't. I guess they both changed their minds.

***

I didn't think wearing orthopedic shoes would help. But I stand corrected.

***

What's the one word you never want to hear a surgeon say?
Oops!

***

I told my doctor I couldn't hear with my left ear.
He said "Are you sure?"
I said "Yes, I'm definite"

***

I did a push up today. Well, actually, I fell down, but I had to use my arms to get up, so . . . you know, close enough.

***

I took a test to see if I was color blind. The doctor reported that the test was inconclusive. He said it was a gray area.

***

Your mind needs exercise just as much as your body does. That's why I think about jogging every day.

***

Drat, I forgot to go to the gym again today; that's 42 years in a row now.

***

This morning I drank water because it's healthy. . . warmed up and poured over coffee grounds. Coffee. I drank coffee.

***

The low-carb diet is the best thing since sliced bread.

***

If God wanted me to touch my toes, he would've put them on my knees.

***

I am a secondhand vegetarian. Cows eat grass. I eat cows.

***

My friend has been diagnosed with kleptomania. Should he take something for it?

***

My friend had one-half of his large intestine removed. I guess you could say that he now has a semi-colon.

***

I'm on a get-healthy program and have started working out religiously. Got the Easter workout behind me, now getting ready for Christmas.

***

Q: What kind of exercises do lazy people do?
A: Diddly-squats

***

I've been hiding from exercise. I'm in the Fitness Protection Program.

***

Wife: I think you need a hearing test. Me: Why would I need a hairy chest?

***

My new exercise regimen:

Jumping to conclusions;
Flying off the handle;
Carrying things too far;
Dodging responsibility;
Pushing my luck;
Climbing the walls,
Dragging my heels;
Bending over backward,
Running around in circles,
Putting my foot in my mouth,
Going over the edge, and
Beating around the bush.

***

I went to the doctor today because every time I drink my morning coffee, I get a stabbing pain in my right eye. He advised me to take the spoon out of the cup first.

***

I have a friend who got rid of her toaster because it kept burning the bread. She said she was black toast intolerant.

***

I switched from lifting free weights to lifting large dictionaries. It gives me more muscle definition.

***

After my physical, my doctor told me: Don't eat anything fatty."
I said: "Do you mean things like bacon and ice cream?"
He said, "No fatty, don't eat anything."

***

I told my psychiatrist I have been having conversations with imaginary people.
He told me: "You don't have a psychiatrist."

***

My deafness has been cured; I never thought I'd hear myself saying that.

***

Yesterday, I burned 2,000 extra calories. That's the last time I leave brownies in the oven w

***

www.ingramcontent.com/pod-product-compliance
Lightning Source LLC
Chambersburg PA
CBHW052013150726
47999CB00004B/1647